TRiM
Sails the Storm

Written by
Deborah Hopkinson

Illustrated by
Kristy Caldwell

PEACHTREE
ATLANTA

For Trim's feline friends, Barlow and Dora,
and their adventurous human family,
Emily, Chad, Sierra, and Clay

—D. H.

For John Michael

—K. C.

Published by
PEACHTREE PUBLISHING COMPANY INC.
1700 Chattahoochee Avenue
Atlanta, Georgia 30318-2112
PeachtreeBooks.com

Text © 2024 by Deborah Hopkinson
Illustrations © 2024 by Kristy Caldwell

Edited by Kathy Landwehr
Design and composition by Lily Steele

The illustrations were rendered with ink, Acryla gouache, colored pencils, and digital tools.

Photo of Trim and Matthew Flinders, Port Lincoln, South Australia
Camloo, CC BY-SA 4.0 *https://creativecommons.org/licenses/by-sa/4.0*,
via Wikimedia Commons

Printed and bound in March 2024 at C&C Offset, Shenzhen, China.
10 9 8 7 6 5 4 3 2 1
First Edition
ISBN: 978-1-68263-292-5

Library of Congress Cataloging-in-Publication Data

Names: Hopkinson, Deborah, author. | Caldwell, Kristy, illustrator.
Title: Trim sails the storm / written by Deborah Hopkinson ; illustrated by Kristy Caldwell.
Description: First edition. | Atlanta : Peachtree, 2024. | Audience: Ages 7-10. | Audience: Grades 2-3. |
Summary: As Trim's first storm starts to rage, his fellow shipmates teach him how to prepare the ship.
Identifiers: LCCN 2023054921 | ISBN 9781682632925 (hardcover) | ISBN 9781682636282 (ebook)
Subjects: CYAC: Cats—Fiction. | Animals—Fiction. | Storms—Fiction. | Sailing ships—Fiction. |
Sea stories. | LCGFT: Animal fiction. |
Readers (Publications)
Classification: LCC PZ7.H778125 Trp 2024 | DDC [Fic]—dc23
LC record available at *https://lccn.loc.gov/2023054921*

Contents

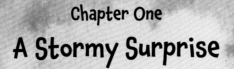

Chapter One
A Stormy Surprise

Trim was a young ship's cat.

He loved to perch on Captain Flinders' shoulder and help Cook in the galley. He liked to watch Will paint in the crow's nest. He even liked patrolling the hold with Princess Bea.

Trim thought he knew all about life at sea.

But he still had a lot to learn.

One morning, Trim trotted out of
the galley and straight into a stormy
surprise.

Wind whipped his whiskers. The sky
was dark and the deck was tilting.
The sails were flap-flap-flapping like
the beating of a drum.

Trim's heart started to beat hard too.

"I'm scared, Penny!" Trim cried.
"Why is the wind so strong?"

"A strong wind tells us a storm is
coming," the ship's dog said.

Trim shivered. "I've never been in
a storm before."

"Don't worry, Trim," Jack said. "We know how to get ready—especially me! I'm a smart bird, a very smart bird. Watch!"

Jack flew to the rigging and screeched,

"Reef the sails, crew!"

"What are the sailors doing, Penny?" Trim asked.

Penny said, "'Reef' means to fold part of a sail to make it smaller."

"Why do they do that?" Trim asked.

"It makes the ship easier to steer in a storm," Penny said.

Trim was glad to learn *one* way to get ready for a storm. Now his heart didn't beat so hard.

1. REEF THE SAILS

Chapter Two
Batten Down the Hatches!

Just then Trim felt a plop.

He mewed in surprise. "Oh, no! It's raining!"

"Don't worry, Trim," Penny said. "We know how to get ready for rain."

Jack screeched, "Batten down the hatches, crew!"

"What are the sailors doing
now, Penny?" Trim asked.

"'Batten' is a strip of wood we use
to cover any openings, or hatches,
on deck," Penny said.

14

"Why?" Trim asked.

"We don't want rain to get into parts of
the ship below," Penny said.

"That's right," Jack said. "Water might
spoil our food supplies in the hold.
Especially my snacks."

Jack began to cover the hatch. "Watch out for leaks, Princess Bea," he called.

"Aye, aye, Jack!" The ship's rat saluted and disappeared below.

Trim was glad to learn *two* ways to get
ready for a storm.

Now his heart didn't beat so hard.

At that moment the captain's
hat blew across the deck.

Will snatched it just in time.

"Thank you, Will," Captain Flinders said. "I've already lost a button today. I don't want to lose my hat too. Time to lash and secure loose items, crew!"

"What are the sailors doing now?"
Trim asked.

"'Lash' means to tie things down. And 'secure'
means to put them away," Penny replied.

"Why?" Trim asked.

"We don't want loose objects sliding around on deck when waves rock the ship," Jack told him. "Something might bump me and rumple my feathers."

Trim was glad to learn *three* ways to get ready for storms.

1. REEF THE SAILS
2. BATTEN DOWN THE HATCHES
3. LASH AND SECURE

"Jack, let's go help the gardener put tools away," Penny said.

Trim's heart began to beat very hard again. Jack and Penny were about to leave him all alone in a storm!

"Wait! What about me?" Trim yowled. "What should I do to get ready?"

"Take cover!" Penny shouted.

"What does that mean?" Trim asked.

"It means to get out of the rain," Penny said.

Jack nodded. "Yes. That's exactly what a cat should do in a storm."

Trim was glad to know *four* ways to get ready for a storm. Especially number four, since his fur was already getting wet.

1. REEF THE SAILS
2. BATTEN DOWN THE HATCHES
3. LASH AND SECURE
4. TAKE COVER

Chapter Three
Trim Helps a New Friend

Trim headed for the galley. Just then he heard a strange sound. He stopped and listened hard.

Screech! Bray! Waahh!

Trim's fur stood on end. Was it the stormy wind? Was it the creaky ship? Or was it a sea monster, washed up from the deep?

The sound came again.

Screech! Bray! Waahh!

Slowly, slowly, Trim peeked around
the corner. He saw a beautiful white bird
with long, black eyebrows and a bit of
pink on her bill.

She wasn't a sea monster at all.

"Hello. I'm Trim, the ship's cat," Trim said.
"Who are you?"

"I'm Wisdom," she said, shaking rain from
her feathers. "I'm an albatross."

Trim asked, "Are you hurt, or sick, or scared of the storm?"

"I'm not hurt or sick," Wisdom said. "I *am* a little bit scared. I'm a young bird and I haven't been in a storm before."

"This is my first storm too," Trim said. "But I think now it's time for us to take cover. That means to get out of the rain. Let's go huddle under that lifeboat. Follow me!"

The storm raged and raged. Trim and Wisdom stayed dry and safe, tucked up under the lifeboat.

Wisdom said, "Thank you for helping me. I still have a lot to learn."

"I do too," Trim said. "My friends showed me four ways to get ready for a storm. But now I know there are *five* ways. Number five is to help someone else stay safe."

After a long while, the rocking ship put Trim and Wisdom to sleep.

Chapter Four
Trim Makes
a Discovery

When Trim woke up, it was dark. The sea was calm and the wind was still. The rain had stopped.

Trim purred. They had made it through the storm!

Trim saw that Wisdom was still sleeping. *My new friend will be hungry when she wakes up*, he thought.

Trim trotted over to the galley. Cook
had put fish stew in his bowl.

Trim plucked a piece of fish and placed
it before Wisdom. She would have a fine
breakfast in the morning.

Trim sat alone
under the twinkling
stars.

One star skittered down
from the dark sky.

Trim blinked. He spied something
shiny nearby.

Had that shooting star landed on their
ship? *No, that's silly*, Trim thought.

Then Trim remembered the captain's
lost silver button.

Trim pounced. "Got it!" He thought, *Captain Flinders will be happy to get this back.*

Trim was still a young cat, but he already knew there are many ways to do something nice for someone else.

Chapter Five
The Best Ship's Cat Ever

The next time Trim woke, the sun was shining in a bright blue sky.

Trim saw the flash of a graceful white wing.

It was Wisdom, gliding over the waves.

Trim hoped he would see his new friend again.

"Oh, what's this?" Captain Flinders picked up the bit of silver. "Look, everyone! Trim found my lost button and kept it safe."

"Hip, hip, hooray for Trim!" the sailors yelled.

"Thanks to all the crew," Captain Flinders said. "We worked together to get ready for the storm. And we came through fine!"

"This calls for honey cakes," Cook said.

Everyone cheered again.

That night, four friends sat on the bow munching honey cakes.

Captain Flinders appeared.

Trim hopped up to his shoulder. It was right where he belonged.

"Tomorrow will be a fine day to explore
the world and learn new things," Captain
Flinders said to Trim. "Are you ready for
more adventures, dear boy?"

Trim purred. He was ready
for anything!

After all, he had sailed the storm,
helped a new friend, and found the
captain's lost button.

I still have a lot to learn, Trim thought.
But I want to be the best ship's cat ever.

And he was.

TRIM SAILS THE STORM is a made-up story about a real cat who lived in the past. We call this kind of story historical fiction.

Trim was born in 1799. Trim's owner was British explorer Matthew Flinders (1774–1814), captain of the HMS *Investigator*. As part of an expedition between 1801 and 1803, Trim became the first cat to sail around the continent of Australia.

The real Trim must have been a brave cat indeed. In August 1803, he and Captain Flinders were shipwrecked on a reef in the Coral Sea Islands, northeast of Queensland, Australia. Captain Flinders tells us that throughout that dreadful night, Trim's "courage was not to be beaten down."

Wisdom (in our story, a Black-browed Albatross common to Australia) was inspired by a real Laysan Albatross named Wisdom. As of 2023, Wisdom was the oldest known wild banded bird in the world.

Captain Flinders told many amazing stories about his beloved cat and called him a "fearless seaman." His tribute to Trim was written in 1809 but was lost until 1971. Today there are statues of these two good friends in England and Australia. And now you know about Trim too.

Matthew Flinders wanted to explore the world because he loved reading sea adventures when he was young. I'll read this story to my cat, Beatrix. I just hope she doesn't decide to run away to sea!

What adventures will you have and write about?

Set Sail with TRiM!

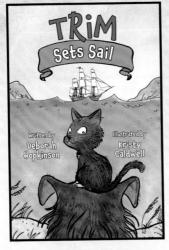

TRiM Sets Sail

Written by Deborah Hopkinson

Illustrated by Kristy Caldwell

HC: 978-1-68263-290-1
PB: 978-1-68263-381-6

TRiM Helps Out

Written by Deborah Hopkinson

Illustrated by Kristy Caldwell

HC: 978-1-68263-291-8
PB: 978-1-68263-382-3

TRiM Saves the Day

Written by Deborah Hopkinson

Illustrated by Kristy Caldwell

HC: 978-1-68263-293-2

TRiM Sails the Storm

Written by Deborah Hopkinson

Illustrated by Kristy Caldwell

HC: 978-1-68263-292-5